THE ADVENTURE ZONE

LEGENDS FROM THE UK

Edited By Kelly Reeves

First published in Great Britain in 2020 by:

Young Writers Est. 1991

Young Writers
Remus House
Coltsfoot Drive
Peterborough
PE2 9BF
Telephone: 01733 890066
Website: www.youngwriters.co.uk

Printed and bound in the UK by BookPrintingUK
Website: www.bookprintinguk.com
YB0437Y

FOREWORD

Welcome, Reader!

Are you ready to enter the Adventure Zone? Then come right this way - your portal to endless new worlds awaits. It's very simple, all you have to do is turn the page and you'll be transported into a wealth of super stories.

Is it magic? Is it a trick? No! It's all down to the skill and imagination of primary school pupils from around the country. We gave them the task of writing a story on any topic, and to do it in just 100 words! I think you'll agree they've achieved that brilliantly – this book is jam-packed with exciting and thrilling tales.

These young authors have brought their ideas to life using only their words. This is the power of creativity and it gives us life too! Here at Young Writers we want to pass our love of the written word onto the next generation and what better way to do that than to celebrate their writing by publishing it in a book!

It sets their work free from homework books and notepads and puts it where it deserves to be – out in the world and preserved forever. Each awesome author in this book should be **super proud** of themselves, and now they've got proof of their ideas and their creativity in black and white, to look back on in years to come!

We hope you enjoy this book as much as we have. Now it's time to let imagination take control, so read on...

CONTENTS

Alicia Moore (10)	61
Tyler Penman (11)	62
Tegan Olivia Kipling (11)	63
Cole Mangles (10)	64
Kaydi Mason (11)	65
Carla Shaw (10)	66
Lucas Weston (10)	67
Joel Price (10)	68
Lydia Knight Hopton (10)	69
Makenzie Cox (11)	70
Lauren Stokoe (10)	71
Tyler Sowerby (10)	72
Jayden Blenkinsopp (11)	73
Ellie Grace Makepeace (10)	74
Scarlett Hatton (11)	75
Elizabeth Randall (10)	76
Molly Wharton (10)	77
Jake Wilkinson (11)	78
Kasey McGregor (10)	79
Luca Randall (10)	80
Leah Hull (11)	81

Crystal Gardens Primary School, Bradford

Zainab Sultan (10)	82
Ruqayyah Ahmed (10)	83
Yahya Sadiq (10)	84
Habiba Khan (10)	85
Safa Bashir (11)	86
Fatimah Bint-Tayyab (10)	87
Suleman Ali (11)	88

Highgate Junior School, Highgate

Ethan Pais (8)	89
Bailey Higgins (7)	90
Ethan McQuaid (8)	91

Hulme Hall Grammar School, Stockport

Aritra Mukherjee (10)	92
Molly Couvela (11)	93
Heidi Eastwood (10)	94
Henry Turner (8)	95
Reuben O'Meara (11)	96

Kittybrewster Primary School, Aberdeen

Zain Almasri (8)	97
Leighton Hanratty (9)	98
Aiesha Hackett (8)	99
Sofia Santos (8)	100
David Knox (7)	101
Kuba Weinerowski (8)	102
Lily Lee Adams (8)	103
Nathan Papka Simduwa (7)	104
Brandon Lee Black (7)	105
Gucio Michal Krauzowicz (8)	106
Josie Wright (8)	107
Ellie Sword (7)	108
Oluwasegun O Ajibose (7)	109
Yusaf Zahmewi	110

Parkfield Community School, Saltley

Hashim Afzaal (11)	111
Ameer Mamundy (10)	112
Jannat Afeel (10)	113
Rumaysa Rehman (10)	114
Sohrob Sidiqi (11)	115
Maria Hanif (10)	116
Maryam Abdullahi (10)	117
Musab Ali (11)	118
Dalia Kamal Ahmad Rostum (10)	119
Sanah Asam (11)	120
Umair Mumtaz (10)	121
Iqra Shafiq (10)	122

Ryecroft CE Middle School, Rocester

Hollie-Mai Laidler (10)	123
Natalie Smith (10)	124
Felicia Mae Jeffery (9)	125
Tom Aubrey (10)	126
Harrison Rai (9)	127
Felicity Johnson (10)	128
Matilda Grace Kent (9)	129
Logan Lewis (9)	130
Lily Stanley (9)	131
Freya Whomersley (9)	132
Kate Turner (10)	133
Edward Bond (9)	134
Annie Cunningham (9)	135
Kian Dowling (9)	136
Jessica Susannah Winship (10)	137
Bethany Palmer (9)	138
Jamie Barr (10)	139
Ellie Emily Stretton (10)	140
Autumn Rose Clamp (10)	141
Anas Terboui (9)	142

St Thomas CE Primary School, Blackburn

Khadijah Nagori (8)	143
Hammad Hussain (7)	144
Mariam Badat (7)	145
Ibrahim Hussain (8)	146
Hawwa Ali (7)	147
Ariana Patel (7)	148
Fatima Shah (8)	149
Mllala Ali (7)	150
Yaseen Zubair Solkar (8)	151
Simrah Waqar (8)	152
Umme-Haani Ayaz (8)	153
Aaishah Mayat (7)	154
Hamza Karbanee (8)	155
Ibrahim Mughal (7)	156
Asad Ul Haq (8)	157
Ismah Nawaz (7)	158
Ayaan Khan (8)	159

Mustafa Hussain (8)	160
Maryam Bari (7)	161
Taibah Sardar (7)	162
Aliyah Aman (7)	163
Ameen Ahmed (7)	164
Hafsa Kalokhe (8)	165
Subhaan Qudeer (7)	166
Furqan Choudhry (8)	167
Mominah Qadir (7)	168
Hamzah Deshmukh (7)	169
Junaid Khan (8)	170
Areefa Tariq (7)	171

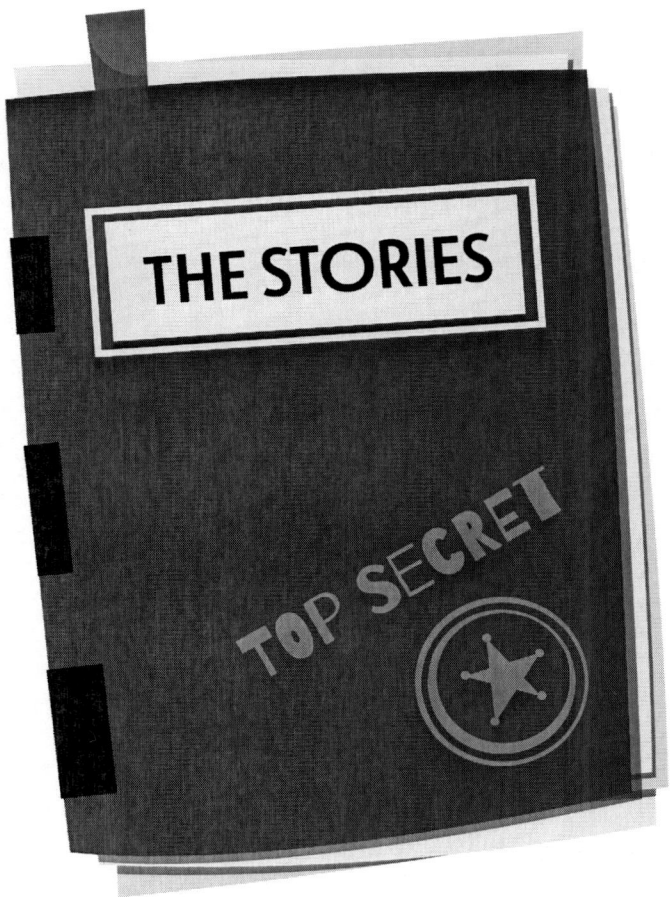

THE STORIES

TOP SECRET

The Big Surprise

Miss Green was upset. It was her birthday and everyone had forgotten. When Alien Super Cop UK-12 heard this, he thought he must do something about it. Everyone should celebrate their birthday, so he began to hatch a plan. He drove around all day, speaking to friends and family, explaining how upset she was. So they all planned a surprise party with balloons, party poppers, tasty food, presents and of course, fireworks. Miss Green loved fireworks. Miss Green's friends even made a huge birthday cake in her favourite colours. They were very excited.
When she arrived, everyone shouted, "Happy birthday!"

Oliver Byles (10)
Bovington Academy, Bovington Camp

Mark's New Planet

Mark was an astronaut, he travelled around different planets a lot. But this time, Mark found a planet near Earth. It was colourful and looked like the Earth. Mark arrived confused, it was so quiet, he was surprised until he took a left.

Green creatures looked up and said, "Goo begoo." Mark stepped back, he turned around and said, "Goo!"

Filled with excitement, all the aliens came to Mark and gave him a big hug. After, Mark left the planet. He named it Green Goo.

A few weeks later, Green Goo became famous and inspired people to go and visit.

Belle Tapping (10)

Bovington Academy, Bovington Camp

Clippy's Christmas

A long time ago, there was a kind man called Clippy. He had a giant heart, full of nice thoughts. That next day, it was Christmas Eve. Every Christmas, Clippy would hand out presents to all of the poor children. That Christmas he couldn't because his brother, Slippy, was taking over. He was evil. Last time he failed, Slippy wanted revenge. When Slippy tried to steal Christmas, the world started to evaporate because children were waking up for nothing. Now just as the world was disappearing, Clippy turned the clocks back and then managed to deliver all of the presents.

Kaison George Justin Chappell (10)

Bovington Academy, Bovington Camp

Fluffy's Wander

A fluffy wolf was wandering along when a mysterious shape-shifter dog jumped out of a spiky bush. The dog, called Scruffy, was disguised as a beautiful female wolf. Fluffy, the real wolf, did not realise that Scruffy wanted to attack him! Fluffy was in deep love with the shape-shifter. So that night, the wolves were in bed. The kind wolf was asleep but Scruffy turned into a disgusting monster who roared with all his might. The noise woke up the tired wolf who howled and sprinted away. The monster couldn't keep up with him. Luckily, the howling wolf was saved.

Bella McAllister (10)
Bovington Academy, Bovington Camp

Detective JB

Suddenly, a fire covered parliament. One man called Jason Banks looked over and saw that prime minister Boris Johnson wasn't there. The detective wanted an opportunity to solve a mystery and now he had one. Then he saw a nearby fire station and asked for a fire engine. But only to put out the fire. After that, Jason needed to find out where Boris Johnson was.

Six hours later, Jason saw handprints on a nearby wall, near Boris' house. He'd never seen anything like this in his career. The worst thing was that the hands were as red as blood...

Ryan Amey (9)
Bovington Academy, Bovington Camp

Nightmare On Christmas

Late at night, Captain Vendemar broke into a mansion, stealing more present from the city's homes. His truck, stolen, was waiting to fly to his secret basement. His machine was ready to bring the toys to life to destroy the city. Super Blink, the city hero, was waiting to catch Captain Vendemar in his trap. He was hiding behind a tree, waiting as Captain Vendemar landed with his truck full of stolen presents. *Bang!* The truck hit the wall. Quickly, he got all the presents and returned them back to their owners. Merry Christmas everyone!

Patrick Thomas Luckman (10)
Bovington Academy, Bovington Camp

The Mystery

One dark, gloomy night, there was an ordinary person watching the news, until he heard that there was a murderer on the loose. He locked his doors and cautiously hid under the bed. Suddenly, he heard people screaming loudly outside. With his heart pounding, he grabbed the phone and called the police. They would be coming. Five minutes later, they were there. He was safe, he heard a loud knock on the door. The police said they caught the murderer and now he was safe.
He said, happily, "Thank you."
He then went off and watched the news.

Isobel Roberts (9)
Bovington Academy, Bovington Camp

The Man And The Monkey

In the morning, there was a monkey in the forest, sleeping on a tree.

There was a man walking, holding his key, then the monkey woke up and he said, "I am hungry."

He saw the man walking and the monkey jumped and took the key. Quickly swinging through the trees, he opened the door and took the man's food. The monkey ran behind the house and ate all of the food. The man came back quickly, to find the monkey in his kitchen. After, the man couldn't find the monkey and he went to bed because he was tired.

Al-Kawthar Al-Aghbari (10)

Bovington Academy, Bovington Camp

The Wonders Of The Doll

Me and my friends went to the park at eight today, it was Christmas Eve. We were about to go when a doll showed up. We stayed still, eye to eye, not knowing what to do.

Nicol said, "It's possessed!"

We all ran home, changed, came back, it was a herd of dolls. Me and Nicol used fire but our powers didn't work. So Mark, Max and Grace used nature but still didn't work. We combined our powers. Nicol: fire, Max: water, Grace: nature, Mark: lightning, me: storm. *Stomp! Boom! Crash!* All of them fell in pieces...

Moses Tuitubou (9)
Bovington Academy, Bovington Camp

The Haunting Of Clara...

Sheral had been haunted by a demon or a spirit called Clara. Clara had been haunting Sheral for two years. Sheral had been going insane for two months. Sheral heard weird and freaky noises at night. Her parents were in a different country but teleported everywhere they went! Clara could go in mirrors and TVs. Did you think Clara would haunt anybody else? The spirit could only see humans, not objects, it was the same for Sheral. Sheral had a terrible life and needed to do something about this matter as soon as possible...

Maddy Amos (9)
Bovington Academy, Bovington Camp

The Tin Soldier

A long time ago, there was a princess called Claire. One day, she found a magical door in her wardrobe and she decided to enter it... She entered into the Christmas tree forest where she found a tin soldier called Phillip. She saw everyone was dark and gloomy. *Bang!* An evil pixie rocked up behind her, trying to turn her into a tin doll and *swoosh!* A sword reflected onto the dark pixie but she already was tin so it hit back at Claire. She was now a tin doll! Would she ever go home or stay here forever?

Ellie-Rose Micklewright (10)
Bovington Academy, Bovington Camp

Unknown Man

Error stepped slowly into the unknown area, Error felt a faint touch. He turned around, nothing. He carried on. Suddenly, he felt blood dripping on his head, he looked up. A head ripped off a body. Error felt a shiver go down his spine then a man stood and stared at him. He did nothing, said nothing and in the blink of an eye, he was frozen. He felt blood coming from his stomach, he fell to the floor then he got a good idea to freeze himself and he did. After a couple of years, humans found him.

Ryan Bood (9)
Bovington Academy, Bovington Camp

Mission Failed

An alien tries to take over the Earth but they are very dumb. They build a machine so they could fly to Earth, so they take over. It takes them to Earth so they can take over Earth, it takes one day to get there. They land on top of a tall building, something is blocking the door but they have windows so they smash the windows. They walk around.
They say, "This needs some work."
The humans scream and the aliens run and hide. They die because they cannot breathe human air.

Jack Somerset (10)
Bovington Academy, Bovington Camp

Candy Land

I stepped through the colourful portal and ended up in a world I'd never seen. I had no idea about what I was. Opening my eyes, I could tell I was in a different world. I was surprised when I saw alive candy! I wanted to try a bit. I took a bit of candyfloss and ate it and then it just disappeared like magic. It seemed like the candy were real people because they could do anything that humans could do. I ate one candy cane and it teleported me back home on my bed where I was before.

Trina Ndzeshu (10)
Bovington Academy, Bovington Camp

My Childhood Dream

I gazed into the distance and saw something weird. I walked over and saw the tiniest puddle ever. I went over, jumped in the puddle and sank. I backed out from the pressure of going to the light. I woke up and the first thing I saw was a giant troll. He told me I had an hour. I was confused, I walked off. I saw dinosaurs that meant they never became extinct! This was amazing. I walked over and the next minute, I was tied up in a chair by a bearded man. This could only mean one thing...

Liam Riley Burt (10)
Bovington Academy, Bovington Camp

Operation Hippo

"Arghhhhhh! Where's my laser blaster gun?" Pasta Guy screamed.

Aliens were coming to Pastaville and Pasta Guy couldn't find his blaster.

"There it is!" he sighed. "Let's get blasting!"

Pasta Guy went zooming through the portal to the street. *Pew! Pew! Bang! Kaboom! Pow! Oof! Pew! Pew! Pew! Rattle! Rattle! Squelch!* He had managed to send them off. Or so he thought...

Suddenly, more aliens came down but there was a slight difference, they were dancing!

Freddie Drakeford (9)
Bovington Academy, Bovington Camp

The Haunted House

I went to my room and it was night. I got into bed and fell asleep. Five minutes later, I heard a strange noise coming from my doll's house.
All my dolls came out and said, "Let's play!"
So I ran down to my mum's room and told her. I fell back asleep but heard it again. My mom saw it too and told my dad. So we hit them with a bat. We saw one and it was possessed with crossed eyes and a cut face with cracks, but finally, we went back to sleep.

Elsie Knapman (9)
Bovington Academy, Bovington Camp

The Darkside Spikes

Gracie stepped through the Darkside, seeing vines, not knowing what would happen. When she turned around, a Spike! As she ran for her life, she remembered Spikes hate circles. Gracie pulled her Coke out and faced the lid at the Spike. Gracie ran towards it whilst it was running and Gracie was heading back to the Brightside and hoping never to come back to the Darkside. As Gracie came out, she still saw vines. There lay before her deep brown eyes... a cracking Spike egg.

Elleigh Louise Smith (9)
Bovington Academy, Bovington Camp

The Exploration

Late at night, a kind guy called Max walked into a forest looking for treasure. He was all alone in the forest. Suddenly, a creature popped out of the bushes. Max jumped back and pulled his sword. His sword sliced the creature's leg as Max was walking. Max realised he was sinking. Max screamed in fear and came up with a plan. He grabbed a tree branch and pulled himself up. When he got out, he tripped over a log then Max realised the treasure was right in front of him.

Michael Walker (9)
Bovington Academy, Bovington Camp

The Missing Unicorns

The unicorns opened a door that they didn't know where it led to. When they opened it, they saw food. The unicorns were surprised when they saw all of the chocolate. They saw sweets that were Twizzlers, candy canes, a chocolate river, regular sweets and a bush of daisies that were nice. The bush daisies really were nice but they made the unicorns float. Then they made them get lost in the middle of nowhere. They didn't like it, they were shocked.

Heidi Batty (9)
Bovington Academy, Bovington Camp

No Wi-Fi

I travelled back in time, to the 1800s, just in time to see a scorching blank desert. I looked around for shelter, but only a single tree was in sight. I sprinted to the tree for my galactic goo ringer (phone). I found it under a baby root, though only to find there was no signal. I remembered the expansion portal, my time machine. Finally, I got out. But, I ended up lost on my own in the unknown.

Aluesi Lawaci (9)
Bovington Academy, Bovington Camp

What Happened To Me

I went through a random portal that sent me into a video game. But it was in real life! I think I had a concussion in my head. Was this a dream? Was I still sleeping in my bed? If only!
This guy stole my soul, but my dad came out of nowhere and saved my life. We had to burrow underground to survive. But the beasts found out that we were burrowed underground so then they ate us.

Tobi Turner (9)
Bovington Academy, Bovington Camp

Clowns Are Alive!

I went to my store and walked through the door and the clown was sat on the floor. I went to the bathroom, they started to dance. I snuck to the cameras, they started stabbing each other, that meant... my toys were alive! I ran out of the store and they did a round of applause.

I went to bed and they were sat right there and said, "Play, play, play!"

Then, I was gone!

Millie Hume (9)
Bovington Academy, Bovington Camp

The Candy Portal

My name is Glittery Jazzy. Whilst playing at my friend Majestic Matilda's, house, we suddenly came across a portal. Surprised yet excited and filled with wonder, we happily stepped inside. Instantly, we were surrounded by colossal candy canes and massive marshmallows. Astonished and hungry, we began to taste them. They were delicious! Feeling full, we wanted to go home and rest. But the portal had vanished! Worried and concerned, we curiously searched around the silent, sweet-filled land. Luckily finding it underneath a jelly bean rainbow, we joyfully skipped through. Although we loved sweets, we didn't want to eat a lot again!

Jasmine Walker (8)
Cheltenham College Prep School, Cheltenham

Magical Forest

Far away, in a magical forest, there lived an enormous, clumsy, yet lonely dinosaur called Jeffry Bobster. All around the beautiful forest, tall yet bulky trees. One dark evening, while Jeffry Bobster was hungrily nibbling on a delicious red apple that had fallen onto the muddly ground, brightness shone down from the moonlight. Shocked and bewildered as a portal suddenly appeared in front of him. Jeffry stumbled and fell into it. Inside the magical portal, Jeffry was surrounded by other dinosaurs. Finally, he had found some friends. Jeffry felt happy at last and he decided to stay there forever.

Alfie Pearson (9)
Cheltenham College Prep School, Cheltenham

Supercats Incorporated - Attack Of The Dogs

I stepped through the portal to find cats flying everywhere.

Before I knew it, a cat swooped down, shouting, "Intruder!"

I was amazed. In this world, cats could talk! The cat led me to a large building that said 'Supercats Inc' in brass letters. When we got there, we met a jet-black cat called Midnight. She asked me who I was and explained that she was the leader of the Supercats. She showed me around the office. There was a desk, a pinboard, an armchair and even a milk dispenser. It was amazing! Suddenly, a cry rang out.

"Dog attack!"

Theodora Rose Walters (9)
Cheltenham College Prep School, Cheltenham

Superheroes

Without thinking, Goku stepped into a portal. There were people flying everywhere. He tried to talk to them but they didn't listen.

Out of nowhere, one of them came up to me and said, "Someone called Lord Fruiza is coming to destroy our planet."

Then he flew off. Suddenly, Goku saw a round object crashing to the ground. It was Fruiza. He morphed quickly.

"Super Saigon power!" he shouted.

His hair turned silver, his top ripped apart. This was called Ultra Instinct. Goku flew into the air, punched it out of space. Goku flew back down.

Kyron Beeston Brown (9)
Cheltenham College Prep School, Cheltenham

Trapped

I jumped off the cliff, not knowing if I'd survive. I did but I was trapped! A massive, freezing, icy wall surrounded me. A roof appeared. I swam around to the edges and tops of the walls to find a way out. None! Petrified, I turned around.
"Shark!" I screamed loudly.
Suffering from hypothermia, I knew I would not survive! The shark had disappeared. Suddenly, I felt a tug. I turned around with another scream to find it was gradually eating my leg, then my body and neck. 'Trapped'. The game time was over. *Beep! Beep! Beep!* I was dead!

Emily Faulkner (9)
Cheltenham College Prep School, Cheltenham

From Myths To Legends

Laughing with joy, I ventured into the dark, blue portal. Before I could say anything about where I was, I was knocked and swept off my feet by a small fox-looking creature. Staring down with enormous fright, I screamed an unbelievably blood-curdling scream. Strangely, my little shabby body was gigantic. Soon, I realised that I had transformed into a beastly cyclops. All of a sudden, I felt an overwhelming pain in both my eyes and my brain. I'd felt this before, I just knew I had. Momentarily, I remembered what it was. I was feeling incredibly faint. Again.
"Nooooo!"

Lula Ramnarine (8)
Cheltenham College Prep School, Cheltenham

Sugar Rush

One morning, my friend, Candy Bella, came round to play. Whilst having fun playing hide-and-seek, Candy Bella suddenly called out to me from the corridor.

"Lula, quick, come here now!"

I hurried to her and was amazed to see before us, a bright purple door. Shocked yet curious, we decided to open it. Insides, sparkles of sugar fell like rain falling from the sky and in front of us was a glittery waterfall. Excited, we rushed over and swam through sugary water. Upon reaching it, we went through, astonishingly arriving back home. Had we dreamt it all?

Lucy Maclean (8)
Cheltenham College Prep School, Cheltenham

Underwater World

I jumped through the glowing portal fearlessly and found myself in a colossal underwater palace. Bravely, I swam through a fancy room - glistening through the window I saw many multicoloured fish: green, orange, red and blue. Something caught my eye! It was a large metal box covered in coral and seaweed. It was impossible to open. As I searched for something to help me, I spotted a combination lock. Excitingly, I twisted the colourful locks. Incredibly, the lock clicked and the lid flew open. I could not believe my eyes. Inside were hundreds of gold coins. I was rich!

Freddie Birch (8)
Cheltenham College Prep School, Cheltenham

The Murder Scene

Cautiously jumping through the devil-black portal, Derick found himself in a murder scene! Noticing yellow caution tape around a dead body, he backed away, hoping it wouldn't be him next in that position. Derick looked behind him and saw, standing in front of him, a tall man dressed head to toe in black! Derick soon became the next victim. Back home, Derick's mother was wondering where he was, she was hoping he hadn't gone through the devil-black portal and not returned like his father. Derick's mum felt a tickly shiver go up her spine and tears fell slowly.

Isla Geary (8)

Cheltenham College Prep School, Cheltenham

The Wild Herd

Galloping across the field, I saw some men in Candy Cane Lane. I stopped Bluebell, my horse. Then I shouted to the men, "What are you doing?" "None of your business!"

A day passed and I hadn't seen the wild herd that I'd been riding with earlier. So I took Bluebell for a ride. Suddenly, I heard a noise coming from them. I was galloping towards them when I saw the men from the day before. They were trying to steal them. Luckily, I had warned the police and they were waiting for them there. The wild horses were free.

Nell Lamyman (9)
Cheltenham College Prep School, Cheltenham

The Girl Who Went Missing

Stepping through a mythical, gloomy portal, before I could take my first breath... *Whoosh! Bang! Pop!* The portal disappeared. Wandering through the creepy, strange world, a biggish creature brushed past me, its skin was as soft as silk. A red beam showered my eyes, I felt as if I was being watched. Within a few seconds, a gloomy, dark shadow towered over me. Its eyes were as red as dark blood, its horn was as sharp as a pin, his hooves shone like butter circling me rapidly. I thought hard and then I realised it was an ugly devil unicorn...

Matilda Grimshaw (9)
Cheltenham College Prep School, Cheltenham

Unicorn Land

Without thinking, I stepped through the bright portal. When I came out the other side, I found a big rainbow touching the ground. Confidently, I went underneath the rainbow into a place which looked like Unicorn Land. There were lots of unicorns and there were some people riding them. "It is so pretty here," I exclaimed to a person, as glitter was falling down.
A unicorn came trotting up to me so I mounted it. The unicorn cantered off with me on and it went through the portal and took me back to my cosy house where I belonged!

Martha Keene (8)
Cheltenham College Prep School, Cheltenham

A Magical Creature!

Confidently, I leapt through the bright sparkling portal. Surrounding me was a dark forest but it didn't look like a normal forest. It looked a bit like a magical forest. I needed to know more. I took one step forward into the dark, magical forest. When something caught the corner of my eye, it was very fast. It looked a bit like a mythical creature. Suddenly, it came out from the shadows. It was a unicorn! I couldn't believe how colourful it was. The unicorn walked so elegantly. Just then, I felt like the most lucky person in the world!

Robyn Bell (9)
Cheltenham College Prep School, Cheltenham

Superhero Adventure

Slowly, Tom stepped through the dark, gloomy portal. Suddenly, he realised that in front of him it was very different, and even the houses looked different too. He had lasers on the front to keep villains away. Eventually, he realised that he'd turned into a superhero, he felt stronger than ever. After a while, Tom discovered that his powers were laser eyes and he could also fly. He felt so happy, but he still wanted to go back to his house in Canada. He had a plan since he could fly. Tom flew up to the portal and shot home safely.

Saif Zaid Jaber (8)
Cheltenham College Prep School, Cheltenham

Monster Danger

Hovering in the air, beside me, I stepped into the black hole, wondering where it would lead. At that moment, there appeared a green jungle with creatures in. Weirdly, they did not seem to make a big deal out of it. There were black ones and even some with one or no eyes. They were happily swinging in the trees, minding their own business. I was feeling scared. The creatures were creepy and terrifying. They were swinging away when through the portal I heard my mum calling me for dinner. So I stepped back, relieved to be out of there.

Sophia Ward (9)
Cheltenham College Prep School, Cheltenham

Fox Devil

Cautiously stepping through the bright, blue portal, I could see tall, dark trees looming above me. Gazing in amazement, a gust of wind brushed past me. Looking down, I saw a foxy-looking bird staring right at me. All of a sudden, a dizzy feeling filled my confused body. It had happened before but not like this. Looking down again, the cute little fox bird had turned into a devil. Screaming with fear, I jumped back, trembling. Back at my house, my mum was hoping that I hadn't disappeared to the fox world that my father had died in!

Seren Harrison (8)
Cheltenham College Prep School, Cheltenham

Lost In The Jungle

Closely and slowly, I stepped into a green, glowing portal, not knowing what I'd find. Loudly, the portal shut dramatically as I stepped into a jungle. I could see big monkeys swooping in the treetops and a refreshing turquoise waterfall with a shoal of fish jumping with excitement. There was a small hut with a thatched roof banging in the treetops. Then, I realised there was no ladder to climb. With a puff of smoke, all my dreams came true so I looked behind me and the portal was gone and only the colourful trees were left.

Olivia Hardwick (9)
Cheltenham College Prep School, Cheltenham

Untitled

Going through the portal, I cautiously looked around. As I stepped forward, I saw a huge eye in front of me and beneath me, sharp pointy teeth. All around me, diamonds glistened and shone. At first, I thought I was in a cave but then I realised I was in the belly of a monster. As I was walking, I saw a huge figure coming towards me. Frightened and scared, I crept towards the creature. While I was walking towards the figure, I got closer, closer and closer. Suddenly, the evil creature pounced at me. What would I do next?

Jack Boyd (9)
Cheltenham College Prep School, Cheltenham

The Unnamed World

I saw a bright blue portal, I stepped inside cautiously. There was caution tape everywhere. I anxiously looked inside, it looked like I was stuck in this disastrous world! Alone, I walked down the vandalised street. A random man shouted my name so I ran as fast as I could down the criminalised street. I missed home so much. The man tapped me on the shoulder so I kicked him hard and ran through the alleyway. It stank of stale food and rats were everywhere. I hid in-between trash cans. I heard the strong man coming...

Archie Hall (9)
Cheltenham College Prep School, Cheltenham

The Last Adventure

Whilst I was slouching down on my sofa, staring at an ugly vase, I felt myself being sucked towards it and before I knew it, I was in a hot and steamy jungle. Amazed by where I was, my first instinct was to get out of there. Anxiously, I was walking through the treacherous rainforest when I came across an interesting river. It was unusual because it had a big boulder with writing on. I read what it said. Unfortunately, in doing so, it exploded into a million pieces. I was in shock and horror. What would he do now?

Herbie Harris (9)

Cheltenham College Prep School, Cheltenham

The Big Difference

Slowly, I wandered into a hot, tree-filled world. There was something slimy attached to me. It was a tentacle. I was covered with them. I hated my body. But... I saw a shard of glass showing my reflection. I was a one-eyed freak! Sobbing in a dark corner, I realised the portal had disappeared into thin air. Suddenly, the trees were closing in around me as if I was trapped in a cage. With no chance of escape, I closed my eyes and everything was gone! I was falling without stopping. I was definitely not going home.

Jasper Penny (8)
Cheltenham College Prep School, Cheltenham

The Land Of Criminals

I stepped into the portal and I shot through it. I flew out of the other side and landed on a pitch-black building. Hanging on with my foot, I saw people robbing banks. Suddenly, I realised I was a superhero. When I sneezed, fire flew out my mouth and I had laser eyes. I tried lasering them but I missed every time. Suddenly, someone kicked me off the edge. Before I thought it was too late, I somehow flew around the town a couple of times and made my way back to the portal and shot back home safely.

Theo Jandyala (9)
Cheltenham College Prep School, Cheltenham

The Wrong World

Watching the space program, Zack was fascinated with it all. He was sitting on his chair. When it showed a picture, he touched it and it turned off and on again. Then he was getting sucked in! Momentarily, he was in a tunnel of bright colours like emerald, ruby and more. When he got to the end, it was space. He could even see the sun from where he was. He looked at where his feet were and it was the moon! He slowly turned and saw his hero, Neil Armstrong. It was a dream come true. Or was it?

Rory Simpson (9)
Cheltenham College Prep School, Cheltenham

Gallop Into A Legend

As I stepped through a purple portal, just then a bunch of feathers hit me in the face! Suddenly, a small pegasus stopped right next to me! I jumped on its back. She took off into the sky. As unsteady as a jelly, I wobbled and fell off. My life flashed before my eyes. When I thought it was all over, I landed in a huge blue lake. Then that's when I thought it was time to go back home! I stepped through the purple portal and... I'm now back right where I started. I'm so happy I'm home now!

Sienna Westwood (8)

Cheltenham College Prep School, Cheltenham

Superhero Land

I stepped through the bright light, not knowing what would happen next. As soon as I stepped through, I knew I was not at home. There were super supermarkets everywhere and what looked like people and dogs zooming through the air like rockets. In the corner of my eye, I noticed a girl shoot into the sky. I wanted to have a go too. So I tried and I tried. Surprisingly, on my last try, I sprang into the air like a jack-in-a-box. But suddenly, I saw the bright light closing up again...

Eva Tabatabai (8)
Cheltenham College Prep School, Cheltenham

Untitled

I stepped into the dark, gloomy hole. As my eyes adjusted, I sat down. The world was dark and round. I could not see a thing but then a strange creature approached and put a mask on my face so that I could see. Then he took me to his friend who had to scan me to see if I had any explosives on me. After that, they took me to a special lab to make my eyes adjust to the darkness of the moon. Eventually, they took me to a moonbuggy to drive around. What an adventure!

Charlie Pritchard (9)
Cheltenham College Prep School, Cheltenham

Don't Stop Walking

I'm on my way home. You wouldn't believe what I have been through. I've trudged through mud, I've been caught in wire, I've been shot at but now I've escaped this treacherous place. Have I told you I'm a horse? The worst part of my journey was crossing no-man's-land, that's when my leg was seriously wounded. I'm nearly there, I'm nearly at hospital. I eventually arrive, I hear a voice. It is my owner, it is my master's son.
He says, "I'm your owner now, my father has died."
He takes me home, we have the greatest time.

Jessica Anne Staples (10)
Cockton Hill Junior School, Cockton Hill

The Mysterious Mighty Monster

An evil monster was terrorising the neighbourhood.
I shouted, "Stop!" but he continued.

They were going crazy. The next day, I went to the
farm to feed my chickens, they were gone. All I
could see was feathers. I sobbed. The monster was
hurting many people, crying and fainting.

He didn't accept money so I got a microphone and
shouted, "Stop hurting the people!"

But it was no use. He put the people down and ran
to the forest to hide. I secretly followed him, he
saw me and started to intimidate me. It was
dangerous and other people died.

Marlee Hopps-Litten (11)
Cockton Hill Junior School, Cockton Hill

Shipwreck

Minutes before the test flight, Ezra started asking all soldiers to step up to it but they would not dare to fly her new light speed engine. To make it more simplified, a girl (Karen) stepped up.

As they lifted off, an unnamed aircraft started to attack, enemies of Ezra, who wanted the millennium and the fuel from the engine. Apparently, it would help them to win the war between the trolls and plaque. They started to shoot Karen and Ezra's ship. Eventually, the ship came crashing down into a forest. This was a new start for Karen's horrible life.

Charlie Bland (11)

Cockton Hill Junior School, Cockton Hill

The Early Birthday Present

I was shaking with excitement when my mam said she was going to give me an early birthday present. Also, I got a choice of which one I wanted to open. I obviously chose the one that was shaped like a video game, who wouldn't?

"Thanks, Mam!" I enthusiastically said.

I loaded it up onto my PS4 quickly. Since it was a game about Roman gladiators, I made my character wear a helmet and armour, with a large shield and sword. I clicked 'Start' and there I was, in an arena. But I wasn't playing the video game anymore...

Freddie Roe (11)
Cockton Hill Junior School, Cockton Hill

A Whole New World!

Without hesitation, I went to check out the weird noise, I approached the neon portal. Hours later, I woke up in a forest. *Where am I?* I thought to myself. But then, I saw a... unicorn! It strolled up to me. Carefully, I stroked the creature. Not soon after, I saw a weird creature approaching me. I thought it was friendly, like the unicorn. But it had an army that attacked me viciously. Luckily, the unicorn stuck by my side, and protected me. Once the creatures were all defeated, I was safe and continued to live with the unicorn happily.

Mischia Hill (11)
Cockton Hill Junior School, Cockton Hill

Under The Sea

I stepped through a bright portal that landed me in the sea with sharks, stingrays and much more. A strange thing, with people inside, was in front of me. I wondered what it was. I went closer to it but a bright flash shot in my eyes. It almost blinded me. *Crash!* It went into the submarine. That's right, a submarine. A strong white shark was there to attack. I was petrified, I didn't know what to do. *Bang!* The evil shark did it again. With my super strength, I swam towards the submarine and was able to save everyone.

Rhys Jay (10)

Cockton Hill Junior School, Cockton Hill

The Carnival Of Death

It was a gloomy night when Elexi attended the colourful carnival. Although this night was like no other, it was colder than before in Indiana Hawkings. Elexi went to play darts while his friend was getting a hot dog. He won a Woody Woodpecker teddy, he was so ecstatic until he turned a corner. *Bang!* Elexi the German was dead. The German who shot him was one of the men who'd been in the Upside Down, a place where creatures can manipulate your mind into becoming a part of their army. Who was Elexi? What happened to the German man?

Maddison Louise Kirtley (11)
Cockton Hill Junior School, Cockton Hill

Inquisitive Eyes

I was ready to go and all fastened up, I finally get to visit Granedove Theatre for my birthday. Hopping out of the car, I saw words carved on the bench next to the reopening theatre. Instead of paying attention to it, I jumped up and down in excitement, looking at the historical building. Still, I couldn't take my eyes off the writing so I walked over and read it. It said, 'Look up', and when I did, there were no people cheering, instead there were ghosts from the past and Granedove Theatre was alight with fiery, large, screaming flames...

Keira Illingworth (11)
Cockton Hill Junior School, Cockton Hill

Death Festival

On the 22nd of September, there was a festival to be held. There would be singing and dancing at the festival. The day had come around. Everyone was pumped up about it except one person who had a murderous plan... Victor! He lived at 101 next to the Smiths. They were petrified of him. Victor's house was dark and gloomy. He had all the potions he could ever ask for.

At the festival, the drinks company was handing out free samples of purple wine but no one knew he'd poisoned the drinks. One by one everyone died, slowly and painfully.

Emilie Peart (10)
Cockton Hill Junior School, Cockton Hill

CD Lands In Town!

Super CD entered a vibrant portal, adjusting his eyes because of the brightness... He quickly entered St Helens and found himself flying around the night sky.

"Oh my gosh!" he shouted nervously, as he passed the ancient school.

As he just found his balance, he twirled and twisted. Suddenly, he spotted a man with a sniper rifle. He twirled over and he kicked the gun out of his hands, snapped it clean in half and called the police. The police rushed, got hold of his slippery arm and threw him into the back of the police van.

Charlie Denham (11)

Cockton Hill Junior School, Cockton Hill

Dino World The Book!

I stepped through a large, colourful portal, it looked different. Same place but more prehistoric. I checked my phone, it was 1.3billion years ago. I stared at my hands. I only had two fingers and claws, I was a dinosaur! I looked around, wow! Volcano! I was surrounded by Velociraptors but when I looked, there were none there. All of a sudden, I was hungry. I found some food but it was alive and my instincts kicked in. I attacked with my bite force... dead! I ate in peace. So I thought... raptors came and so I battled with them.

Lucas Peverley (11)
Cockton Hill Junior School, Cockton Hill

The Bright Portal Into The Unknown

I was in my bedroom until a bright portal opened up and I stepped into it. Thoughts whirled around my head and there was a distant singing. Next thing I knew, I was in an unusual world. The sky, which was iridescent, had a shining sun which shone over a beautiful castle. It wasn't long before I realised I was far from home and stood in the middle of nowhere with only shops, stalls, forests and castles. I was willing to do anything just to be back home. I was exhausted and thirsty, I felt myself beginning to lose consciousness...

Alicia Moore (10)

Cockton Hill Junior School, Cockton Hill

Mission: Deliver The Pizza!

It was a normal day, I was driving the pizza-mobile to deliver for an unspecified location. Not a big deal, I would just follow the map! Soon, I was driving on a straight concrete road with no streetlights or signs. *Boom!* I fell into a pit of burning, bubbling magma. All of a sudden, I was caught by a mysterious force and I was sucked into a parallel universe. I was unconscious but I could see everything. I could see myself sleeping! Was I in an astral dream? Everyone was some sort of food and I was yummy chicken pizza.

Tyler Penman (11)
Cockton Hill Junior School, Cockton Hill

BBQ Pizza Delivery

Pizza delivery! I needed to deliver a pizza to another dimension, The McFlurry Dimension. I was cycling down the road when suddenly, I fell into a bright light. Endlessly spinning around, I fell to the floor and when I looked up, I was amazed. Houses were covered in ice cream and sprinkles. I got up and cycled around for what seemed like forever. Eventually, I gave up, but suddenly, I realised that my map was online. This place was somewhere on the route. Once I had got to the end of the map, I was at my destination, early.

Tegan Olivia Kipling (11)
Cockton Hill Junior School, Cockton Hill

Writers® Est. 1991

Top Gun

My name is Goose, I work for Top Gun Fantastia's. I've just finished my new jet, I'm ready to battle. Flying this Brazil would take a while but with infinite fuel, it will be fine. When I sneakily got in the invasion arena, they'd seem me. Sending all their jets after me, I called for back-up. Back-up arrived, the battle had begun. We got rid of them but more came. The missions were going to take me out if I didn't do something. Astonishingly, we lifted the base with more back-up. We ran away, we'd won the war. Party time!

Cole Mangles (10)
Cockton Hill Junior School, Cockton Hill

64

The Mystery Bookshelf

One evening, I decided to read a book, but the book I had chosen unlocked a secret passageway. The next thing I knew, I was sucked through a portal... Whizzing round and round in circles, I suddenly dropped to the ground. Carefully, I opened my eyes. Monsters and ghosts were filling the place with fright. Skeletons lay on the ground and kids and adults were running round the place, screaming. My mouth dropped in terror, what would I do? My heart beat faster. I saw a house nearby and I ran towards it, the door slammed...

Kaydi Mason (11)
Cockton Hill Junior School, Cockton Hill

The Horror Ghost

The tree was finally decorated as I heard a girl sweetly singing. I lived alone, I checked everywhere. Suddenly, the cupboard doors opened. I was sucked in, screaming. A portal! When I landed, people were walking through me. How? A voice was telling me, *kill!* With a fury inside me, I got up and ran for a kid. I felt bad, I couldn't stop. Suddenly, my head turned to a little girl. No! Before I knew it, she was dead. It was kid after kid. After a devastating onslaught, I was sucked back home. I sat and cried.

Carla Shaw (10)
Cockton Hill Junior School, Cockton Hill

The Mystery Of The Theatre

Leaving the theatre, I heard a sinister voice, "Four doors, which will it be? One contains some lava, one contains a murderer, one contains school and the last one... a mystery portal."
Hating school and knowing lava and a murderer would kill me, mystery portal it was! *Bark!* Where did that come from? I realised that I was a black and white spotty dog. I was so confused. Nose to the ground, I sniffed my way to an old farm. Excitedly, I saw another dog, a girl dog, and bounded towards her...

Lucas Weston (10)
Cockton Hill Junior School, Cockton Hill

Blown By Bane

Inquisitively, I stepped through the mysterious, luminous portal. All I knew was that I had become Bane, the masked man, and I had evil intentions to destroy Batman and blow up Gotham General Hospital, where Jim Gordon was recovering from a recent sniper shot that had hit his weak, old left shoulder. It was then I realised where I was. I was in an armoury as if I was ready to strike! Gotham was about to change and it wasn't for the better... What was I doing? I couldn't but I didn't think I had a choice. Did I?

Joel Price (10)
Cockton Hill Junior School, Cockton Hill

The Wardrobe To A Secret Land

Hello, this is the whole extraordinary story about how I managed to enter a land of mythical creatures. As usual, I went to my wardrobe to get my PJs and there was a galaxy-coloured portal waiting for me to enter, so I did. I felt like I was in a whirlpool of water. When I got there, it was a land of mythical creatures with unicorns, fairies and rainbows. It wasn't a coincidence all of my favourite colours, pink, blue and purple, were there. Suddenly, the unicorn came up to me and placed a crown on my head.

Lydia Knight Hopton (10)
Cockton Hill Junior School, Cockton Hill

The Story Of The Missing Girl

It all started when I was decorating my Christmas tree. Suddenly, it came to life and I was sucked into a portal. I ended up in a world called Whoville. I was a green, furry creature called Ronald. Eventually, I came across a little girl called Sindy-Lue and we became friends. We were having fun but she was kidnapped. Quickly, I chased them to get Sindy back but it was so hard to catch them because I was tired. However, I remembered I had two sweets so I ate them. I got my friend back but I was passed out.

Makenzie Cox (11)
Cockton Hill Junior School, Cockton Hill

Fluffy

One morning, after collecting the post, I found a letter for me so I opened it. The next thing I knew, I was a huge, grey, fluffy, three-headed dog and in a strange place. Also, when I arrived, I was taken to a bank called Gringotts to protect it. Nervously, a man called Rubeus Hagrid came to collect me every weekend to let me have fun and get away from the slanted bank. However, one day, I didn't have to go to work. Instead, I was locked away in a deep, dark and gloomy dungeon. What was going to happen?

Lauren Stokoe (10)
Cockton Hill Junior School, Cockton Hill

The Hero And The Thief

One bright and early morning, I was in the middle of playing a board game when I heard a strange sound. Stood in front of me was a twisted hole. The portal was very gloomy and loud. I didn't know what was inside. Suddenly, I went to go and see what was in the portal. When I arrived, it was an enormous city full of tall towers, up to 100-feet high. I saw something horrendous - a criminal. I needed to catch him so I targeted him, he was in jail now. I thought, *my majestic powers strike again!*

Tyler Sowerby (10)
Cockton Hill Junior School, Cockton Hill

The Mysterious Forest

Alone on the island, I was exhausted because I had been walking for hours. Searching for food and water. No joy, I found some coconuts on top of palm trees. I climbed up. I took a nap. I felt like crying because I was so scared and terrified, thinking I would die. A day had passed, I started to search for water again. Luckily, I found a lake and drank from it. It was like heaven. Finally, I had something to drink. At least I would survive now with food and water. I thought I could get used to this.

Jayden Blenkinsopp (11)
Cockton Hill Junior School, Cockton Hill

Mermaid Magic

At the beach, I was having fun. Excitedly, I ran towards the cool water. All of a sudden, I felt a sharp pull as I was dragged under the water. I had gone through a portal. I was able to breathe and suddenly, I realised I was a beautiful mermaid. I tried to find some mermaids but couldn't. Finally, a mermaid came up to me and told me about the king and queen of the sea. I swam around in the quiet sea, watching the colourful fish. I felt happy because I liked being underwater. I decided to stay.

Ellie Grace Makepeace (10)
Cockton Hill Junior School, Cockton Hill

Detective Evie Queen And The Isle Of The Lost

Hello there, my name is Evie Queen. My day started like it always did, at school. Even though I'm royal, people bully me, it's not nice. When school finished, there was a huge portal that was so magnetic. I wasn't sure where I was headed but the colours hypnotised me. When I came out the other side, there was a whole mystery for me to solve. There was a villain, who was stealing Maleficent's stuff. At first, I wondered why but with a load of clues, we caught her. A strange sound began to echo...

Scarlett Hatton (11)
Cockton Hill Junior School, Cockton Hill

Shape-Shifter's Secret

I knew I shouldn't have told them but I thought we would be BFFs no matter what. Here is how it all started... Like normal, I went to school, it was a boring day. However, after school, I went to Britisha and Elisha's house for a sleepover. After supper, we had Pot Noodles. By the way, I told them my secret! I told them that I was a shape-shifter. Two days later, everyone knew my secret and they all thought I was an alien. I'm so heartbroken, I'll never forgive them!

Elizabeth Randall (10)
Cockton Hill Junior School, Cockton Hill

We All Fall Down

In just a minute, I had fallen into a dark room with cameras of what seemed to be live videos of New York City. After a while, I understood that I was a villain, I knew it was wrong but I was too inquisitive. My mission was to blow up NYC at 12am at night. I was ready. A couple of hours passed by.
"I am ready to do this!" I said to myself.
I called my best friend to tell her about this crime but she said I shouldn't do it. It was time to strike, but... should I?

Molly Wharton (10)
Cockton Hill Junior School, Cockton Hill

Goodbye Friend. Goodbye.

For ten years, my best mate has been Chris. We both work in the army as fighter jet pilots. It is 2019, World War III is just beginning, and me and Chris are the best at speaking German so our mission is to work as spies.

One wild, windy night, we manage to get in the German base and we know what they are up to. They are planning to get the jet and bomb the trench in the dark but there is a problem, there is only one jet. We steal the jet, but Chris falls...

Jake Wilkinson (11)
Cockton Hill Junior School, Cockton Hill

Amazing Ponies

Bright portal eyes adjusted with feathery velociraptor ponies everywhere. There were ponies clinging to lampposts. Ponies grazed on the grass and the roof. Special ponies were the best animals because they were only the best of the best of animals on Earth. They were very friendly and nice to humans and when they were only three weeks old, they started to eat solid food and ran in the wild at nine months old. I realised I had to take really good care of her.

Kasey McGregor (10)
Cockton Hill Junior School, Cockton Hill

The Wild Aliens!

One day, I saw a weird portal and it said, 'Area 51', so I went and I got food and water and went through. It was magical! It made me into an alien and I sat down in the portal and it made me green. My eyes were black. The portal had an alien on and it took me to a desert and it showed a picture of aliens, and there were other aliens on the fence. It was dark and when the sun came up, it made the aliens go into the bunker.

Luca Randall (10)
Cockton Hill Junior School, Cockton Hill

My Toys Are Alive!

One strange morning, I was in my bedroom and a magical portal appeared, waiting for me to explore. I was eager to go inside and as soon as I did, it was an exact replica of my bedroom! The strange thing was my toys were alive! I thought to myself, *I am going to be famous*, but then realised nobody would believe me. My toys were now surrounding me! I screamed for help but nobody could hear me!

Leah Hull (11)
Cockton Hill Junior School, Cockton Hill

Haunted House

Two brothers and sisters found an old video game and decided to play it. When they plugged it in, the plug gave little sparks of fire. They turned the switch off but they were sucked into the video game. They found themselves in a haunted house. "Where are we?" asked Jessie.

"I don't know," said Max.

They carried on moving along the narrow corridors when a skeleton dressed as a bride chased them. They found a door, went in.

In the room they saw a vampire but also a little hole. They went in and were back in their bedroom.

Zainab Sultan (10)
Crystal Gardens Primary School, Bradford

Night Nightmare

On the deep, dark hill, there was a spooky house. Charlie, his mum and dad were a very rich family. They could also afford a lot of things.

One day, Charlie's mother said to him, "Go out and find me some leaves please."

So off Charlie went. Suddenly, Charlie heard a strange noise and his eyes became bloodshot. He carried on doing what he was doing but still heard peculiar noises. The walls started to become towering and Charlie was very scared so off he went inside his house with a spiderweb dangling down. He was never seen again.

Ruqayyah Ahmed (10)
Crystal Gardens Primary School, Bradford

Horror Boy

"Mum, I need help!" screamed Joe. "The front door is stuck!"
"Coming!" shouted Mum. "And where are you going, young man?"
"Harry's house."
"And who were you going to ask?"
"You don't, erm... have a dad."
"Bye! Fine, bye!"
Harry and Joe were playing outside. *Thump!* Mum screamed then a thud. An atrocious being fell on the floor. Was it a ghost or a boy? Harry said it was both. Then Horror Boy, that is what we named him, threw a cube on the floor. Me and Harry suited up and jumped in. We entered a gloomy place.

Yahya Sadiq (10)
Crystal Gardens Primary School, Bradford

The Ghost That Leads Two Children Into The Future

Under the apple tree, the two friends went to get some apples to make apple juice.

"What was that?" they called in a scared voice.

Then they heard a voice saying, "I'm going to get you."

As the two friends were moving further, the voice was coming closer. Then the two kids hid, they saw a ghost that was saying the spooky things. Then the ghost grabbed both children and dragged them into a purple circle that was glowing. It led them into the future and they saw people that looked weird and now they were in the TV.

Habiba Khan (10)
Crystal Gardens Primary School, Bradford

Future Saved

Sam was exploring Neptune as part of her mission when a silver object came speeding towards her. It landed and a door opened. Four aliens stepped out. They clutched Sam and dragged her into their aircraft and flew into a black hole. Sam looked around. They were on another planet and there were aliens everywhere. The aliens told her that she was in the future. He told her that a meteor was going to hit Earth. Sam knew what to do. She got in the spaceship and charged for the meteor. It burst into several pieces. Earth was saved.

Safa Bashir (11)
Crystal Gardens Primary School, Bradford

The Tunnel

One dark, murky day, Chloe was on her way back from school when she saw a peculiar-looking creature. She decided to follow it. She ran like a mad maniac until she realised she was lost. Chloe was in a large spooky forest. A low, creepy moan was heard. All of a sudden, a tree trunk opened up and swallowed Chloe. She let out a blood-curdling scream as she whizzed through a tunnel. She found a ginormous ghost who gave her a satnav to find her way home.
"If you come here again, I will eat you!"
Chloe ran off.

Fatimah Bint-Tayyab (10)
Crystal Gardens Primary School, Bradford

Bullied

There was a boy who was bullied every day, he was always depressed, he tried to take the depression away by creating a Ouija board. He played it, but nothing happened. About one hour later, it was midnight, he heard a noise. He peeked outside his window, only to see a tall man staring directly at him. The boy went under his bed, hoping not to see the tall man again. He looked in the hallways only to see the tall man looking in every bedroom. The boy went under his bed, something grabbed his foot and he was there...

Suleman Ali (11)
Crystal Gardens Primary School, Bradford

The Hunt Of The Asian Diamond

"When's Jo going to come?"
"I've been waiting for days."
Finally, Jo came.
"Are you ready for the Asian diamond?" Kit asked.
They went to Hello PC in Israel. When they went in, they saw scary creatures: mummies, werewolves and lots more. It was super scary. They checked tiles and all the furniture but there was no sight of the diamond. They both wondered if the creatures could be a clue. So they asked every creature if they knew where the diamond was but they had no clue. They thought even harder but they had nothing. It was a mystery...

Ethan Pais (8)
Highgate Junior School, Highgate

The Fight For Atlantic

In the lost forest of Atlantic, lived funny little creatures called Clownbows and TBs. Clownbows could change colour depending on their mood and could control the weather. It was a typical day in the Atlantic, the air was clear and the water flowed and the fruit was plentiful. Until an army of men marched in and started chopping down trees and polluting the water. This upset the Clownbows and TBs. They turned dark black and it started to rain. It didn't stop for weeks, forcing the men to leave. When they left, the rain stopped. They panicked on the boat.

Bailey Higgins (7)
Highgate Junior School, Highgate

Lost In Edinburgh!

Once upon a time, a bear called Bob, and his family were up Ben Nevis, eating. Suddenly a speedy avalanche started and they got separated, The parents were together but sadly, baby Bob was not. He went looking for them, but he had to sleep. Just then, he saw some smoke, he went to it and two people were there. They took him into their house. He had lots of fun, they went on walks, hikes and runs. Still, Bob could not get his mind off his family. But one day, he saw a way out...

Ethan McQuaid (8)
Highgate Junior School, Highgate

The Story Of The Ori And Elementals

Long before time had a name, there was a realm of Elementals and Oris. The Oris had the power to destroy the Elementals. One day, a man was born with both powers and they fought over which side he should be on. He was banished to a different universe with one Ori and one Elemental to guard his son, Leo.

"Wait, you're telling me I can control the Elementals and Ori?

"Yes, the Ori betrayed your father and wanted to get you. I am your protector and brother..."

Suddenly, Leo heard a sound, it was the Ori...

Aritra Mukherjee (10)
Hulme Hall Grammar School, Stockport

The Grizzly Monster

Once there was a horrible, grizzly monster that wanted to rule the world! Isobel is our heroine who saved the day. Isobel had long, black, silky hair and blue eyes... The grizzly monster had a body like a snake, if he touched you, you'd die in four minutes. Driving to work, Isobel heard a bang. A massive dent was in her car. She drove to work, objects flew around the room. She was frozen to the spot! She picked up the broom and started hitting aimlessly around the room. Her boss walked in. "What are you doing? You look crazy!"

Molly Couvela (11)
Hulme Hall Grammar School, Stockport

Laughter Is The Best Medicine

Once in a dark cave, there was a sad beast called Happy. He shouldn't be happy, he should be called Sadness.

Seven years later, after seven years of being lonely, he said to himself, "I want to look for a friend."

So he set off to a land called Bewic. He went into the candyfloss shop and the shopkeeper was very kind. His name was Springy. Happy had never seen anything so colourful as Springy. His eyes were blue and pink. He hopped like a bunny. This made Happy laugh and they are still friends today.

Heidi Eastwood (10)

Hulme Hall Grammar School, Stockport

Laser Man

Laser Man was not an ordinary man, he had X-ray eyes that could see into a person's heart. He had cannons for ears, which could cause serious injury and a blade on his head that was permanently attached. So he looked a bit like a helicopter. He could hover in the air and take off and land instantly. He could jump higher than a skyscraper. He killed all the monsters except for one. The Devil of Destruction kept on destroying buildings. Laser Man shot the Devil of Destruction with a laser beam. Laser Man saved the world.

Henry Turner (8)
Hulme Hall Grammar School, Stockport

The Last Stand

The year was 4100, it was a time of war. The Zeds were taking over the universe, enslaving, killing and putting the civilians to work. I was organising a SWAT team to overpower the Zeds. I am Quantum. Currently, I was on a high outpost on the edge of the Thames. A massive claw rushed out of the water, grabbed me and hurled me at a space freighter. I landed with a thwack on the ground and formed a crater with the impact. I heard a laser, it hit me and everything went black! Was this the end? Hopefully not!

Reuben O'Meara (11)
Hulme Hall Grammar School, Stockport

Cyber Man Into The Universe!

Once upon an amazing time, there was a superhero called Cyber Man. He could shoot webs, robotic system attack and more. One night in London, something strange happened.
Cyber Man said, "What is that?"
It was... Electro.
Cyber Man said, "Electro, long time no see."
Electro said, "Hello Cyber Man."
They started to fight! Electro was all made out of electricity. Cyber Man was made out of systems. The fight took 100 minutes and finally, the fight finished and Electro finally died.
Cyber Man said, "Phew! Finally that's over!"
Cyber Man went home, back to New York.

Zain Almasri (8)
Kittybrewster Primary School, Aberdeen

Far Away In Dinosaur Land

Once upon a time, there was a dinosaur land that was very dark and scary. Lots of huge creatures lived there. Every day they were chasing the humans. Everybody was terrified of them. One lucky day, the superhero arrived. He was very powerful and had lots of superpowers. His name was Kevin. When he found out that the dinosaurs were horrible to the poor people, he decided to help them. Kevin used his superpowers to help him to paralyse the creatures. He came towards them and used his laser to save the world from those horrible and scary creatures.

Leighton Hanratty (9)

Kittybrewster Primary School, Aberdeen

No Colours Left

I was taking a walk in Colour Town. Suddenly, Colour Taker started taking all the colours away. I wasn't going to let that happen. I came out. I had to save the day with my happy superpowers to get all the colours back. The town had to be happy again. Colour Taker was extremely angry. He was going mental, taking the colours away. But happiness was stronger than anger. The more angry he was, the weaker he was and the weaker his powers became. Suddenly, he couldn't move. I put all the colours back in Colour Town with my happy powers.

Aiesha Hackett (8)
Kittybrewster Primary School, Aberdeen

Santa Went Missing!

One day, I was travelling to a cold place. My parents only told me that.

When we got there, I said, "Where?"

"In the North Pole."

I went for a walk and saw Santa's workshop. I went inside to find Santa. I looked everywhere, he wasn't there. I put on my detective clothes and I was investigating where Santa went. I asked Miss Claus if she'd seen him.

"I saw him checking on the sleigh."

I went to go and see, I saw his footprints. They went to the kitchen. There was Santa!

Sofia Santos (8)

Kittybrewster Primary School, Aberdeen

The Jungle

Me and Brandon and Yusef and Zain were in the jungle. We saw a snake and we ran into a cave. We were frightened and scared to move.

Next day, we crept out and I saw a massive scary tiger sleeping in the long grass. We tiptoed past him so that we didn't wake him up. Suddenly he yawned and we saw his wide-opened mouth with long sharp teeth.

"Time to escape, it is getting way too dangerous!" shouted Zain. "Look, there's a boat!"

We ran as fast as we could and jumped into the canoe. We paddled to safety.

David Knox (7)
Kittybrewster Primary School, Aberdeen

The Mystery On The Cruise Ship

Once upon a time, there was a ship full of chests of treasure, diamonds and money.
Months later some pieces of gold disappeared but three pieces of gold had been dropped on the floor. All crew tried to find who the robber was. The dropped pieces led towards the sea. The captain looked out of the ship and saw some coins floating in the water. It was a big mystery for everybody. A sailor dove into the deep sea to solve this mystery. He saw a mermaid playing happily with their coins and took them back to the ship.

Kuba Weinerowski (8)
Kittybrewster Primary School, Aberdeen

Mystery Of The Lost Soul

The girl is called Leine and she is a detective who solves cases. Leine doesn't ask people if she can solve it, she just does it and always solves it each and every time, but this time, it is very tricky. Someone murdered her cousin and she has to solve who did it. She has been trying. *Boom!* She falls deep under the ground, there are tunnels and tunnels but she didn't dig them. They don't look like humans dug them, so she is running and running for miles. She bumps into something, it is a Buttycorn...

Lily Lee Adams (8)
Kittybrewster Primary School, Aberdeen

Going To Candyland (Very Violent)

Once upon a time, an alien went to save Candy Land. First, he turned into Green Lantern. Second, he had to teleport. He was scared at first. But later, he did it. He teleported to Candy Land. When he arrived, he was amazed. He killed some aliens. Then he heard some gunshots. He teleported north, Candy Land was near to death! People were sad, aliens were happy. Green Lantern was very sad and angry. There was a big battle of fifty versus one. Green Lantern won and they lived happily ever after.

Nathan Papka Simduwa (7)
Kittybrewster Primary School, Aberdeen

The Dark Night

It was a dark, scary Halloween night and we were out trick or treating. All of a sudden a creepy ghost and aliens with green spiky bodies appeared in the sky. I was terrified. I couldn't believe my eyes. I started to run away and suddenly I fell in a big hole. It was dark, cold and muddy. I was freaked out. I felt trapped. I pulled myself up out of the hole and the ghost with aliens were chasing me around the town. I saw some trash cans and I jumped in and closed the lid. Safe at last!

Brandon Lee Black (7)
Kittybrewster Primary School, Aberdeen

Lego Worlds

I went into the portal and it went to a world of Lego, but most of all, Lego cars! Any car you could imagine from A-Z, from Audi to Ford, and Ford to much more. They even had the smallest car in the world! The Peel P50! Oh my goodness, what did I see? The Lego car set I wanted since 2015! The Ford F-150 Raptor with a Ford Hot Rod on a trailer and garage, but more than that, a Mustang sports car. Wow! Well, I couldn't stay here. Now, where was that portal? There it was. Goodbye.

Gucio Michal Krauzowicz (8)

Kittybrewster Primary School, Aberdeen

The Suspicious Sloth

One day, we were out in Slothville to see Sid, my sloth, in his office. We had a five-minute chat. Next, we went to the zoo and we saw another sloth called Sophia. I even got to hold her. The next day, me and Sophia had swapped places. All of a sudden, I became the little sloth and Sophia was a human. I realised that this all happened because I held her! Although I was a sloth, I was still able to talk like a human. Sid came to me and helped me to get back to normal magically.

Josie Wright (8)
Kittybrewster Primary School, Aberdeen

The Enchanted Forest

One day, I saw a big light. I went to see what it was, it was a portal. I went into the portal, I was in a forest. It was an enchanted forest. I saw unicorns and leprechauns. It was so pretty. I was riding on the unicorns, the leprechauns had so much gold. It was time to have a party. We danced all night, there was food and drinks. It was the best night ever, but it was time for me to go back home. I went back in the portal. I had the best time ever.

Ellie Sword (7)
Kittybrewster Primary School, Aberdeen

Tim The Cat

Tim the Cat is a superhero. Today, he had a battle with a giant toilet, he fell into the toilet and he got powers. He got a spray and then turned invisible. He got faster. He couldn't believe it, he lost his powers. He went back in time and his powers were restored. He ran and ran until he got home. He was happy, and then ran into the road. He stopped, then rushed back into the room. He stopped. He could now fly, but he still couldn't swim.

Oluwasegun O Ajibose (7)
Kittybrewster Primary School, Aberdeen

The Jungle Journey

Me and Brandon and David went to the jungle. We were making a campfire. When we slept, we saw a baby tiger. He did not have sharp teeth. Two years later, I met the same tiger and he had pointy and sharp teeth. I felt scared because he had dragon teeth and I found him in the enchanted mountain. He showed me his mountain. There were one billion and twenty thousand tigers. The big tiger was the king of all the tigers and everybody was happy.

Yusaf Zahmewi
Kittybrewster Primary School, Aberdeen

Jokeland

Layne searched left and right until he found it. *The portal's here*, he thought.

"Goodbye Planet Earth and hello Jokeland!" Layne yelled out.

He stepped in. It was... well... home for him. A man popped up.

"Hey, hey, buddy, how you doing? Things get muddy like the flowers blooming. My name is Mike and I ride a bike!" he exclaimed.

"Nice to meet you! I'm Layne Joker!" Layne replied. He took his hand out. Mike shook it. They both got electrocuted.

"You must know my trick, Layne?" Mike asked.

"Sure thing! I'm a pro at pranks!" Layne replied, looking down.

Hashim Afzaal (11)
Parkfield Community School, Saltley

Dragon Ball

Bang!

"S-Sayain Pod!"

"Hey Gohan, we're got a problem."

A mysterious figure was standing. As the dust cleared, Goku had seen a Sayain tail.

"Why are you here?" said Gohan.

"I have come for your planet, now surrender or we can do this the hard way. Make a decision!" replied the stranger with a dull voice.

"Never, you can't come and take our planet with no reason," said Goku.

"Hey Dad, check out his battle power," said Gohan with shock.

"943trillion, that's incredible!" said Goku.

The battle for Namek had begun.

Ameer Mamundy (10)

Parkfield Community School, Saltley

The Doorway...

Creak went the floorboards as I slowly crept along them. I was treading carefully along, trying not to make a sound. A bead of sweat dripped down my forehead. I thought to myself, *what am I doing here?* I regretted playing truth or dare with Mason, especially on Hallow's Eve. He had dared me to go to Old Man Jenkins' house, which was rumoured to have unnatural beings inside. *Scratch!* I stood frozen... A mouldy, tattered door stood in front of me, I peered into the keyhole. But... it sucked me inside! I screamed but nobody answered. I was trapped...

Jannat Afeel (10)
Parkfield Community School, Saltley

Leukaemia

Bang! Geroge fell as he was playing. Despite being ill with leukaemia, he was strong. His parents found him, still on the floor. He was rushed to hospital. Sadly, he found out he was getting worse and was going to die soon. His beloved parents cried fountains of tears. He was going to stop having treatment until a doctor named Peter rushed in the room and told him not to be heartbroken. This spectacular doctor told his parents he could make medicine to make him better. He spent several nights making the medicine. He tried it on George. It worked!

Rumaysa Rehman (10)
Parkfield Community School, Saltley

The Robbery Of The Stolen Jewels!

One day at the Western City, it was okay, everyone was having a great time (not), until a robbery had happened and everyone knew who it was. It was Sir Robby, the greatest mastermind in the world! There was one person for the job, Sohrob, the incredible detective and superhero! He could stop five villains in a day. But this one was very sneaky and very smart. Furthermore, Sohrob looked for him. Fortunately, he saw Robby running. Unfortunately, he disappeared, but the money bag was there. Sadly, the cops came and arrested him because he had the bag...

Sohrob Sidiqi (11)
Parkfield Community School, Saltley

Stranded On A Desert Island

Yawn! I woke with a scream. I was surrounded by wavy water.

"Hi, I'm a scientist. I have just created a new dimension. It seems to be an island surrounded by water, I need to investigate this awesome invention."

I walked along the beach, urged to move until I saw ice. It was heading towards the island. I didn't want my creation destroyed so I did whatever I could but nothing would work until it turned another direction, so I followed it. When I turned the corner, it was gone. The iceberg hit the Titanic and that's how it happened.

Maria Hanif (10)

Parkfield Community School, Saltley

Back From The Dead

There they were. Two men wearing expensive designer suits, carrying a revolver. It was a hot summer's day and was quite unusual to see rich men in these parts. The men turned into a dark, desolate alleyway, jabbering in rapid Spanish. Lurking in the shadows, was a thin, well-nourished boy with fair hair and startling green eyes darting from side to side. Little did they know he had been taught Spanish at the age of seven, along with many other languages. It dawned on him what they were talking about. It was his father. He was really and truly alive!

Maryam Abdullahi (10)
Parkfield Community School, Saltley

The Theft

As James stood there with police at every corner, he surrendered. With his brother dead, he had no choice. As he put the drugs down, he reluctantly went inside the police car. As they went, the gangs came out of hiding and ran. Cluelessly, they didn't know that the cars that looked normal were not. They were running into undercover, armed police. As the police got out, they were cornered. Rapidly, the police got out their guns, poised them at the gangs. A flash of light came, blinding the police. Quickly, the gangs got in the car and ran away.

Musab Ali (11)
Parkfield Community School, Saltley

What I Heard!

I am Lily Parker, well actually that's the name I'm known as. My real name is Alexa Steel. I go with that name as my dad was a double agent, working for both good and bad, but he's dead now, all due to his cruel betrayal to both sides. My mum is a mystery, I have not a clue where she is...
I was walking from school when an alert-looking man rapidly rushed past me. This was weird, so I followed him to a pathway!
A lady walked past saying, "Is Alexa Steel really here?"
Suddenly, there was silence...

Dalia Kamal Ahmad Rostum (10)
Parkfield Community School, Saltley

My Toys Are Alive!

It was Nikki's birthday, she was now turning eight. Moreover, her mother was going out to buy her some presents which were: a doll, a mini make-up set and a new bike. The next day, Nikki was so surprised at the presents she got. As she opened the last present, she was so happy that her mom finally bought her a make-up set. As she piled up her toys, she heard a little voice.

"Who was that?" Nikki whispered to herself. She looked at her dolls.

"Hello," said the doll with yellow hair.

"Arghhhhh!" Nikki screamed.

Sanah Asam (11)
Parkfield Community School, Saltley

A Halloween Nightmare!

There was a care home full of children who had gone on holiday to Japan but there were two children left behind. They saw an abandoned house, they went in the house which had cracks and was broken. There were two dolls which had blood dripping down their faces. There was a strange noise from the attic which was rusty and old. They saw a... ghost! One screamed and then fainted, Her sister was running as fast as she could... she tripped over a pile of books. She broke her ankle. She knew that her life was over.

Umair Mumtaz (10)
Parkfield Community School, Saltley

Clueless Mystery

As I walked through the dark, musty forest, I stumbled across a dark, dirty cottage. I looked to the left, I looked to the right. There in the corner of my eye, I saw the letter 'L'. A part of me wanted to run away but I forced myself to go inside. I glanced for a second. There, in the corner of the shadows of darkness, I saw a skeleton. I screamed and cried as the walls caved in on me. Then I realised the body was none other than my friend, Lucy. She was dead and I was alone.

Iqra Shafiq (10)
Parkfield Community School, Saltley

Henry Trotter And The Battle Of The Thestrals And Unicorns

One gloomy day, Henry Trotter was walking through a dark, mystic forest, when he saw the most peculiar sight. What was it? Suddenly, unicorn blood spilt at his feet. He looked up and saw a Thestral and unicorn fighting. Quickly, he separated them and jumped onto the Thestral's back. He flew to Wartclaw to tell Doredumble what had happened. Doredumble listened to his every word. When Henry finished talking, Doredumble jumped to his feet and set off towards the forest. He froze the Thestrals and unicorns and gave one to Henry, then he separated the rest into different lands forever.

Hollie-Mai Laidler (10)
Ryecroft CE Middle School, Rocester

Save The Sea

One day, Mia, the elegant mermaid, was on her way to visit Nancy, her pet narwhal. Nancy lived in the deepest depths of the Pacific Ocean. Therefore it was a long way to get there. As Mia was on her way, she saw something dreadful. There was rubbish everywhere.

"Oh no, look there is a young starfish, we have to help it. It's got stuck in a large bit of plastic and it's about to suffocate!"

"We need some help!"

"Help! Help!"

"What about Nancy? I haven't seen her in ages. I need to save her and the sea."

Natalie Smith (10)

Ryecroft CE Middle School, Rocester

Murder Maid 2

One day, Murder Maid was playing with Mia and Alivia. They got bored after a while so they went to the real world. Everyone was friendly but if someone spoke to them, they would kill them. Fishy turned into a dog while the others turned into evil unicorns. They had black hair, red horns and wings like the darkest night. They went to the happy shack. *Bang!* People saw that the person who was at the till was dead. Dramatically, Murder Maid appeared, shooting scales from her tail. Running away quickly, people were worried and wondered when she would stop.

Felicia Mae Jeffery (9)
Ryecroft CE Middle School, Rocester

Down In The Creepy Castle

Once there was a young, handsome prince who was jealous and unkind. One night, in the middle of a dance, an old woman entered the castle and gave the prince a rose. The prince laughed and ordered the musicians to play again. However, the old woman was angry and wanted revenge. The woman suddenly turned into a really pale ghost and cursed a spell on everybody in the castle. She turned everyone into horrifying ghosts!

The woman said, "If you be kind, the spell will be broken. If not, you'll remain as a ghost forever!" Would he learn?

Tom Aubrey (10)
Ryecroft CE Middle School, Rocester

The Friends

Once upon a time, there were four friends, they were called Blob, Red Knight, Black Knight and Pelly. They were mucking about on their speed-boosters, buggies, planes and robots. Then two people came, they all got out of their vehicles. The stranger said, "Come with us."

"No!" they replied.

Then the strangers got guns out so they all got back into their vehicles. They split up. The strangers called back-up, two more strangers came. They were all chasing them, we were about to lose hope, then Club Team Leader came out to catch the baddies.

Harrison Rai (9)
Ryecroft CE Middle School, Rocester

It's Christmas Time!

Ring! Ring! The phone went. Zara picked it up. "Hello?"

Someone reported a sleigh of some sort. Zara asked for the place, name and if anything was beeping. She sent some officers to search for the sleigh. A few minutes later, the phone rang. An officer reported a sighting of the sleigh. Zara felt very excited as she had stopped believing. Back at the sleigh site, an old lady sat on a bench. Suddenly, Santa strolled past, got on his sleigh and drove off into the moonlit sky. When Zara was told the story, she was gobsmacked.

Felicity Johnson (10)
Ryecroft CE Middle School, Rocester

Candy Land

One day, there was a girl with a dog called Fluffy. She was called Matilda. Matilda loved a good adventure. One day, Fluffy and Matilda found a portal and when they were through, they entered Candy Land. There was pink candyfloss clouds and lollipop trees, a candy cane forest and doughnut caves so they went into the doughnut cave. But then they found a unicorn and named it Rainbow. They decided to live in the cave but Fluffy bit some of the cave. So they had to call up the chocolate boat and jumped up on the boat.
"Bye-bye!"

Matilda Grace Kent (9)
Ryecroft CE Middle School, Rocester

Alien Experiments

One day, an alien experiment was taking place at Area 51. Alien 1 was his name - the test officer said it couldn't go wrong but it did. In the dead of night, he escaped. In the morning, the main test officer walked in. The alien wasn't there. Tom, the test officer, felt anxious. He saw Alien 1 on the floor, eating a poor cat. He turned around and just stared. Tom looked away and then looked back to find himself floating. His neck kept bending and bending until... *crack!* The next day, Dan, the policeman, went the same way.

Logan Lewis (9)
Ryecroft CE Middle School, Rocester

The Underwater Kingdom

One day, me and my unicorn were called to go to the fish kingdom. They had lots of fish going missing. Then we got on our diving gear and down we went. When we arrived, we went straight to the king. We started searching and came across a cave.

I knocked and said, "Are you home?"

A croaky voice said, "Come in."

We walked in and saw all the fish, including the sea witch, sleeping. So we picked all the locks and set the fish free. We received medals of honour. We partied all night. We lived happily ever after.

Lily Stanley (9)
Ryecroft CE Middle School, Rocester

Ellie The Superhero Saves The Day!

Once there lived an alien called Gobbel. He lived in a spaceship in the Milky Way. One day, something very bad happened, he lost control of his steering and he was heading straight for the burning, hot sun. He needed help and fast! Meanwhile, back on Earth, a girl called Ellie heard a rumbling sound. Now, Ellie wasn't a normal girl, she was a superhero. She grabbed her cape and put it on. With a stamp of her feet, she was gone, shooting up to the spaceship. She hopped on board and steered it out the way. Gobbel was saved!

Freya Whomersley (9)
Ryecroft CE Middle School, Rocester

Bog

Bog was a dragon who was young. His skin was an amber colour and his eyes were blue. Bog had a problem, he was being bullied by kids at Dragon School. Bog always dreamed of breathing fire one day, so Bog set off on an adventure to the closest volcano to collect some fire. Finally, Bog reached the top and looked at the lava. It was really hot. Bog opened his mouth wide and swallowed a big gulp of lava. Nothing changed, all was quiet. Suddenly, Bog started coughing and spluttering, then a bolt of fire came. Bog was happy.

Kate Turner (10)
Ryecroft CE Middle School, Rocester

Mythical Madness

Once upon a time, there was a deep, dark forest with wolves and other creatures in the woods, one was a basilisk. One person went to look for it, his name was Eddie. With his dusty truck, he went into the woods, not knowing it was the most feared of its time. Suddenly, he found a shedding of a big snake.

"It must be close," whispered Eddie.

He heard hissing, he crept closer. There it was, huge and slimy. It heard him. Quickly, he put his foot on the pedal and got out of the deep, dark, creepy woods.

Edward Bond (9)
Ryecroft CE Middle School, Rocester

Bubbles' Loss!

Sea was causing trouble again so Bubbles was in town. But something might go wrong! In the museum, Sea had broken the Statue of Earth, one of the most powerful superheroes. Bubbles put Sea in a bubble and she went up to space. Bubbles followed. *Pop* went the bubble. Sea got out, she flew in the air and Bubbles' bubbles ran out. They got in a big fight! Sea ripped Bubbles' cape! She needed her cape to fly so slowly, she started to fall. Sea laughed and Bubbles fell to the floor. Would she get back up?

Annie Cunningham (9)
Ryecroft CE Middle School, Rocester

Aliens Destroy The World

There were aliens that wanted to take over the world, but we wouldn't let them do that. They are ugly aliens, uglier than ugly, so ugly that everyone was scared of them. So they went in their UFO and tried to kill the king and queen. Zooming, they went 600mph and the police were after them. The king and queen went after them as well but the ugly aliens had a laser which they started using to destroy the world, everyone and everything in it. Eventually, they took over the world and destroyed everything.

Kian Dowling (9)
Ryecroft CE Middle School, Rocester

The Girl Who Owned A Unicat

One day in Candy Land, a girl walked down Cotton Avenue with a swirly candy cone in her small hand. Suddenly, she saw a ginger cat which surprisingly had rainbow hair. The girl, who was called Rosie, ran in excitement after the unusual cat. After running for what felt like hours, Rosie managed to leap forwards and grab the cat who had a gleaming horn in-between its fluffy ears. The cat wriggled and jiggled until realising that Rosie was a good and understanding owner for the unicat.

Jessica Susannah Winship (10)

Ryecroft CE Middle School, Rocester

Jewels

Once upon a time, there lived a girl called Freya. She was a detective and it was her job to get back the jewels. Off she went on a mission to find them, but on her way, she saw a wolf. He dragged her away and wanted to boil her for tea as she looked delicious.

"Yum yum," whispered the mean wolf.

Suddenly, scared Freya saw an old door. Looking at the cruel wolf, she ran and leapt through the door. Before her eyes, she saw the stolen jewels twinkling like stars...

Bethany Palmer (9)
Ryecroft CE Middle School, Rocester

The Suspicious Mystery

I was in my shadowy and gloomy office when I heard a creak next door. I went round to see if anything or anyone was there. I saw a shadow. I was horrified at this moment, but as brave as an army man going into war. As quick as I saw it, it was gone. I found the shadow in my office, but this time it looked bigger. I tried chasing it, but it was too fast. I tried to chase it again and again until the moment of truth. I caught it finally! It was a ferociously humongous rat!

Jamie Barr (10)
Ryecroft CE Middle School, Rocester

Bobble And The Villain

Once there was a dog called Bobble, he was walking across the roadwalk and all of a sudden, an alien called Freya appeared. She was a slimy, terrible villain. Bobble was so scared, she cried and screamed to try and get help. But she couldn't get any help, no one was about that day. But all of a sudden, Bobble was in a green, weird UFO. There were so many buttons. Bobble just wanted to touch them all. But then Bobble fell out of the UFO and he was back at his house.

Ellie Emily Stretton (10)
Ryecroft CE Middle School, Rocester

A Christmas Eve Adventure

Creeping down the stairs, I heard bells jingling and I saw a red jacket. I thought it was Santa because it was 25th December. My teddy and my brother ran all the way to the alleyway. The man had disappeared. We didn't know where he went, then we looked above ourr heads and saw the sleigh. We got a camera and filmed it by climbing onto a car and jumping into the sleigh. Father Christmas came back and we sat where the toys were and off we went with Santa.

Autumn Rose Clamp (10)
Ryecroft CE Middle School, Rocester

The Rainbow Flying Pig

Once upon a time, there was a pig, he was rainbow-coloured. He found a jetpack and filled the tank up with lava. His friends made fun of him, because he was little and he wasn't like the other pigs. He didn't care about them though, he was proud of his rainbow skin. The jetpack had wings! He was a flying pig. The other pigs were jealous and mad. They tried to catch him, but they couldn't because he flew up into the midnight sky.

Anas Terboui (9)
Ryecroft CE Middle School, Rocester

The Adventurous Day

Redhead and Kristy went to Turkey to skydive. They were nervous, they had never been to Turkey. Stomach churning. Body trembling. Hands shaking. Redhead, who was scared of heights, could not believe how Kristy was busy taking a selfie, putting in enormous words before hashtag Turkey. Two hours later, they were over a mountain, how cool! Kristy noticed that Redhead was snoring on her. Then she shouted, "Wake up!"
Suddenly, the balloon popped and floated to the ground. They explored the island, they found a sign. It said, 'If you find a cloud, we will help you'...

Khadijah Nagori (8)
St Thomas CE Primary School, Blackburn

Georgy's Great Adventure

Georgy started climbing to fulfil his dream but the weather didn't help. It was raining heavily and becoming very windy. He gripped tight to keep safe but the wind was getting stronger. There were little bits flying everywhere. Georgy was worried and scared that he was going to fall. All of a sudden, Georgy lost grip and started falling and lost control of himself. But luckily, his backpack got caught on a branch of a tree. The branch broke off the tree but fortunately, he managed to jump to a safe landing. Georgy realised that climbing hills was not easy.

Hammad Hussain (7)
St Thomas CE Primary School, Blackburn

The Miracle

There was once a little boy called Mikle and he had a bad disease and he went around the world to many hospitals, however, they couldn't do anything to help him.

One night, he was dreaming about his grandmother who passed away. She said to Mikle, "Go to Barren Mountain and there will be a blue plant and you should eat it."

He went with his friend to Barren Mountain. Mikle found the blue plant and ate it. Miraculously, he started to get better.

When he got home, his parents were so shocked. Now he plays with his friends.

Mariam Badat (7)
St Thomas CE Primary School, Blackburn

Cool Mr Softy

Mr Softy got a metal detector and went to the beach and he saw orange, soft sand and the water rippling. He could also see people making sandcastles. His shiny metal detector led him to a golden crown. It also had blue, red and green diamonds on it. The queen sent guards out to find it. Suddenly, the guards saw Mr Softy and the crown. Mr Softy also saw the guards and he ran backwards but another group of guards were there.

Mr Softy bumped into the guards and they said, "Hand over the shiny, golden, silvery, heavy, excellent crown!"

Ibrahim Hussain (8)
St Thomas CE Primary School, Blackburn

On A Yeti

One stormy day, Wonderous Woman climbed up to the top.
She said, panting, "That was a long climb."
She could see a breath-taking view and she said, "This is a nice view. I want to stay here."
Abruptly, the mountains were breaking.
She said, "What is that? I don't know what is happening."
She realised that she wasn't on a mountain, she was on a yeti. Then she whistled to get some creatures. But the yeti liked Wonderous Woman and the yeti cried. But Wonderous Woman liked the yeti as well so they went on adventures.

Hawwa Ali (7)
St Thomas CE Primary School, Blackburn

The Ghost

One icy, snowy day, Sophie and Tom excitedly ran out of their house and started to travel around the woods. On their way, they saw something enchanted glowing. In the spur of the moment, they started rising up. They were in a place where the sun was shining in a bright yellow condition. The clouds were as fluffy as fluffy snow. They were astonished! All at once, they felt two wrinkly hands grabbing them. Their hearts started to tremble. They shook their heads and they were no longer being grabbed by anyone. Blissfully, they were back home.

Ariana Patel (7)
St Thomas CE Primary School, Blackburn

In The Forest

Once upon a time, there was a boy called Jack and he loved to explore, but his mum always said, "No!" So one night, he went to the forest behind his garden. He packed his bag and descended into the forest. As he walked on and on, the creatures and animals made him tremble with fear, his heart was beating faster than a cheetah. Then there was a noise and he scuttled.

The boy said, "Run and never come back."

So he ran away. When he was home, the sun was moving.

"Never mind," he said.

"Breakfast time," said Mum.

Fatima Shah (8)

St Thomas CE Primary School, Blackburn

Mystery Adventure

Once upon a time, there was a girl called Supherah. Supherah was on a beach in Turkey. She was walking across the beach. Suddenly, she fell on a rock. Supherah saw something glowing, she saw a ring. The great Supherah fell into a black hole. The great Supherah found a gem, she landed on some sand where some people grabbed her by her body. The great Supherah ended up at a forest where the people tied her around a rope on a tree. The great Supherah's friend found her and unwrapped her.

She said, "Thank you so much."

Mllala Ali (7)

St Thomas CE Primary School, Blackburn

Greg And The Zombie

Greg had finally climbed to the top. He could see the incredible view and the beautiful blue sea, the fluffy clouds. But then, some man took him away. Then Greg had to start climbing down the mountain. He felt something. He looked around, he saw there was a black hole. The black hole sucked him up into a forest. He started walking in the middle of the distance. Greg looked around, he saw a zombie. Greg started as fast as an Audi R8. Greg kept on going. He saw a black door, he had finally escaped. What an exhausting adventure!

Yaseen Zubair Solkar (8)
St Thomas CE Primary School, Blackburn

Fantastic Lusy And Her Adventure

Fantastic Lusy eventually reached somewhere where there was a nice view. Lusy was exhausted, her heart was beating so fast. She could see the view. She could see castles and rocks. The beautiful sky was there. Suddenly, she felt a hand touch her. Then unexpectedly, her hands were wrapped with Sellotape and in her mouth was some hot chilli. She was taken into a box with nothing to eat or drink. Then all at once, she disappeared. But the door of the car was open and the box fell on the witch with Lusy in it. Then she got out.

Simrah Waqar (8)

St Thomas CE Primary School, Blackburn

A Mystery Story

One snowy day, Amazing Alisha was climbing on the hill. She looked above her. She saw the clouds, fluffy as cotton candy. She looked below her. She saw a string of money and said, "Yay!" She went running down the hill. The money was moving but Alisha ran along. Then she saw a van and she stepped inside. A big man looked at her in the van. He switched the van light on. She screamed as she was panicking. Then she realised it was her dad. He opened the door, her family stood outside. They wished her a happy birthday.

Umme-Haani Ayaz (8)
St Thomas CE Primary School, Blackburn

Owerlet

One day, early in the morning, Owerlet drove up a spooky, rocky mountain. She was excited because her family was with her. But then, she heard a sound. She was screaming! She was nearly going to fall out of the car. She hurt herself so her family rushed to help her. They all helped her. She got up and carried on driving slowly. They were nearly there, but Owerlet was hungry, so she ate her lunch.

Finally, they reached the top of the spooky and rocky mountain. She was really nervous, but then she was not scared at all.

Aaishah Mayat (7)
St Thomas CE Primary School, Blackburn

The Mystery

One stormy day, Amazing James was skydiving above a mountain. Below him he could see the ocean. Above him, he could see clouds. He saw two men coming to grab him. Amazing James landed on the mountain with the two men. Abruptly, they took all his belongings and put it in the car. He ran quickly but the car was too fast. He went to get his bike to find the car, and get his stuff. He followed the car marks around the mountain. He found a door, with his stuff inside. Amazing James quickly took them and he left.

Hamza Karbanee (8)
St Thomas CE Primary School, Blackburn

Detective And The Lost Bag

One night, Detective said the forest came to life. He was living in a tiny cottage. After five minutes, winter was approaching and the naked trees were trembling. The cottage was full of fluffy snow. He went outside, he was frozen ice. He couldn't move. He was stuck, ice-still. He could not move an inch. Slowly he became free, then he ran as fast as he could. He forgot something outside. He ran, there were hailstones falling from the air. Finally, everything stopped. He went to the forest, he was stuck.

Ibrahim Mughal (7)
St Thomas CE Primary School, Blackburn

The Mysterious Day

One windy, snowy day when the naked trees were trembling, there lived a rich boy called Dantom. One day, when the snow was coming as fast as a cheetah, Dantom was going to the gym. He decided to run because he wanted more energy. When he was running, he saw the gym and it was enormous. Suddenly, he saw a stranger with a dark scratch on his face. He grabbed Dantom and gave him sleeping pills. The next day, Dantom woke up and he was on the tallest mountain he'd ever seen and the sharpest mountain too...

Asad Ul Haq (8)

St Thomas CE Primary School, Blackburn

Kidnapped

One gloomy day, there was a girl called Saira. She went to a place that was beautiful and high. She looked up at the bright sky and fluffy clouds. Suddenly, she found money on the floor then someone from the black Jeep kidnapped her. They put a black bag over her. She tried to escape but she found she could not escape. She found a key on the floor and picked it up. She opened the door then she escaped. The kidnappers were chasing Saira. They could not catch up to her. So they went back to the black Jeep.

Ismah Nawaz (7)
St Thomas CE Primary School, Blackburn

The Muck Monster's Revenge

There was a village. A man made a monster, a very small one. When he added water, it grew and grew until the same night, it attacked him and sent him to the sewers. He went the opposite direction, he came back for his revenge.

"Roar!" said the Muck Monster, with his sweaty mouth.

He said, "I will get you all!"

Then came a dragon from nowhere, the Muck Monster versus the dragon. He fired the hall and the village. The Muck Monster melted and was gone for good but the dragon died too sadly.

Ayaan Khan (8)

St Thomas CE Primary School, Blackburn

The Story Of Deckard, Luke And Dom

Deckard Shaw robbed the Natwest bank with his friends, Luke Hobbs and Dominic Torreto. Off they went to rob the bank. When they went, they saw a murderer ready to kill them. Dom, Luke and Shaw were not scared at all so they killed him.

Luke said, "Guys, I think we are the murderers."

They all went to prison. When it was visiting time, the boss of the person that they killed was there. They stayed in jail for longer. They were very upset and so were their sad mums, dads and wives.

Mustafa Hussain (8)

St Thomas CE Primary School, Blackburn

A Mystery Story

One snowy day, Amazing Ariana finally climbed right to the top. Suddenly, her heart was beating fast. She could not believe she did it. But when she saw the snowy mountain, she had a think. How did she do it? She realised that she wasn't quite at the top so she climbed some more. That was a long climb. After a few moments, she felt tired, so she wanted some rest, so she had a rest.
It was morning and she got up and she saw her house, so she went to her house and lived happily ever after.

Maryam Bari (7)
St Thomas CE Primary School, Blackburn

Cat Girl And The Mystery Man

One snowy night, Cat Girl was on a creepy adventure. Whilst she was on the adventure, a mystery man came behind her. She was afraid. Then after, she stopped on a mystery road. When Cat Girl got on the creepy, scary road, she saw a creepy house. After nine minutes, Cat Girl decided to go in the creepy house. When she went into the house, she found a dead body in the creepy house. When she found the dead body, she was afraid, she was so afraid that she ran out of the creepy house. She was confused.

Taibah Sardar (7)
St Thomas CE Primary School, Blackburn

The Terrific Story

One bright, sparkly day, amazing Aliyah and beautiful Aidah were bored. They decided to go somewhere beautiful, somewhere with a lovely sea. It was the beach. It was so nice. All of a sudden, amazing Aliyah and beautiful Aidah felt like someone was following them. So they looked back and there was no one there. After a while, they got home, they were all alone at home. So they locked the door and ran into their room and hid in their blankets. They were so scared. What a strange day it was.

Aliyah Aman (7)
St Thomas CE Primary School, Blackburn

The Great Thunder

One foggy day, Pika Mouse Man came out of his cave and finally reached it. Without warning, thunder struck him again and again until Pika Mouse Man finally was able to dodge it. Out of the blue, Pika Mouse Man felt a hand dragging in his cave. It didn't feel like his roommate's so he wasn't sure anyone else knew where he lived. The man told him to pray to God for powers to stop the thunder that was sent. When he prayed to God, he was able to stop the thunder and he lived well.

Ameen Ahmed (7)
St Thomas CE Primary School, Blackburn

A Mysterious Day

Amazing Umaina finally reached right to the top. She was so exhausted she nearly fell. Luckily, she had ice-cold water. She sat down and rested. All of a sudden, someone grabbed her. She screamed right to the top of her voice but no one heard her. Someone began to tie her hands tightly. They threw her into a bag. She felt the truck moving. She realised she had scissors, she cut the bag open and ran away. What a mysterious day she had. No one ever knew where she went.

Hafsa Kalokhe (8)
St Thomas CE Primary School, Blackburn

Malignant Spectre

Once upon a time, lived a beast named the Iron Beast and only three people dared to fight him. Who were these three people? You think I will tell you their names...?
Okay.
Their names were Percy, Harry and Gecko.
People thought it was a myth because there had been no proof. But now they had to face the Iron Beast and they went to battle and Percy had the last strike. So the three friends defeated the Iron Beast and returned to their city.

Subhaan Qudeer (7)
St Thomas CE Primary School, Blackburn

Jan Robinson

One scary night, a man was approaching a forest.
His name was Jan Robinson, he finally got out.
He said, "Yes!"
His friends were surprised but he did not care about his friends.
His friend said, "What? Why?"
"Because you trapped me in that forest."
"We did not trap you," they argued.
Jan said, "Stop!"
"Why?"
"Look what it has done to us."
"You're right."
"Should we be friends again?"
"We should."

Furqan Choudhry (8)
St Thomas CE Primary School, Blackburn

Aliyah And Lucy

Aliyah was looking for a place to sit but she got kidnapped. They blindfolded her and put her in a car and drove off. They locked the car and she invited her friend, Lucy, but she couldn't find her. She called Aliyah but she didn't answer. She went to her house but she wasn't there. And Aliyah was tied up. But the boot was open. She couldn't see, she screamed and Lucy heard her and Lucy ran to her. Then she unblindfolded Aliyah and untied her.

Mominah Qadir (7)
St Thomas CE Primary School, Blackburn

Don't Get Trapped

One fine day, Warrior Man was walking around three enormous mountains. Next to the three mountains, there was a tree the size of a sixty-foot yeti. The leaves on it were as long as the claws of a sloth. After he saw that, he heard a creaking sound, then saw something green with piggy eyes near the mountain. He crept closer to it. Suddenly he fell into a hole in the ground. It was a trap. Out of nowhere, a bat pulled him out of the ground...

Hamzah Deshmukh (7)
St Thomas CE Primary School, Blackburn

In The Spooky House

Once upon a time, there was a man called Jake. He went to the spooky house. Jake got kidnapped. There was a spider crawling up the wall. He was scared. The man gave him some water but it was snowing and it was windy. The man left Jake, he was sad. The man came back, he gave him some food and drink. He let him have a break, they tied him up. They gave him some sweets and chocolate. They set him free, he was happy they let him go.

Junaid Khan (8)
St Thomas CE Primary School, Blackburn

Amirah's Worst Dream!

Amirah had been kidnapped in a spooky car. When they reached their destination, she couldn't see a glimpse of anyone at first, but just then, she saw a smelly and ugly-looking witch. When she saw her, she locked her up in a room. She tried to escape but couldn't escape because there were cameras all over the place.

When she woke up, it was all a dream.

Areefa Tariq (7)
St Thomas CE Primary School, Blackburn

YoungWriters®
Est. 1991

YOUNG WRITERS
INFORMATION

We hope you have enjoyed reading this book – and that you will continue to in the coming years.

If you're a young writer who enjoys reading and creative writing, or the parent of an enthusiastic poet or story writer, do visit our website **www.youngwriters.co.uk**. Here you will find free competitions, workshops and games, as well as recommended reads, a poetry glossary and our blog. There's lots to keep budding writers motivated to write!

If you would like to order further copies of this book, or any of our other titles, then please give us a call or order via your online account.

Young Writers
Remus House
Coltsfoot Drive
Peterborough
PE2 9BF
(01733) 890066
info@youngwriters.co.uk

Join in the conversation!
Tips, news, giveaways and much more!

f YoungWritersUK   **🐦** @YoungWritersCW